Disney

100

YEARS OF WONDER

Storybook Collection

Disney PRESS

LOS ANGELES · NEW YORK

CONTENTS

For information address Disney Press, 1200 Grand Central Avenue, Glendale, California 91201.

Printed in the United States of America
First Hardcover Edition, October 2023

10 9 8 7 6 5 4 3 2 1

This book is set in 14-point Baskerville MT Pro.

Editor: Lori Campos
Designer: Julie Rose
Cover Art Lead: Caroline Egan

Library of Congress Control Number: 2023931126

ISBN 978-1-368-08393-5
FAC-034274-23236

Visit www.disneybooks.com

From **PETE DOCTER**

Chief Creative Officer, Pixar Animation Studios

"WONDER" is a funny word.

It reminds me of bread.

It reminds me of lunch. As in "I wonder what we're having for lunch." (I wonder about lunch a lot.)

But mostly, wonder reminds me of a feeling. It's a feeling I got when a magician made coins disappear right in front of my eyes. Another time I felt it when I was at a lake and a giant flock of birds flew overhead. And last spring when tiny bright green plants pushed up through the wet dirt, sprouting from dried-up seeds.

At these times it feels like my brain is widening, and I feel my skin tingle. My mouth drops open and my eyes get stuck. I'm right there in that moment, not thinking about a mistake I made yesterday or things I have to do tomorrow. It's a feeling I wish I had more often.

That's probably why so many of us at Pixar try to create that feeling in our movies. It's tricky to find that magic combination of elements that make you feel that way. Sometimes it comes from something huge or majestic, like when Lightning McQueen turns a corner to see a waterfall in Ornament Valley. Other times it's sparked by something that seems impossible, like Carl Fredricksen lifting his house into the sky with balloons. Or it could come from someone you've known for a long time but now see in a new way, like when Marlin finally rescues Nemo after swimming across the ocean.

Thinking about it logically, I'm not really sure what reason there is for wonder. Does it help humanity? Does a sense of wonder make us more likely to hunt down dinner? Or to pass along our genes to future generations?

Another weird thing about wonder: it can be found in stuff that you see every day, but that you somehow see differently. Like, yesterday, when I saw an ant crawling across my kitchen counter, I squished it. Then today I saw one, and I stopped and stared, amazed that something so small could have a sense of purpose and personality.

As unexplained as it is, wonder does help us remember that we live in a pretty amazing world. And it's there anytime you want—all you have to do is stop and look for it. Wonder does make life better.

Kind of like lunch.

THE WONDER OF
FAMILY

"Whenever you feel alone, just remember that those kings will always be there to guide you. And so will I."

—*Mufasa*

THE
LION KING

SIMBA WAS A MISCHIEVOUS little lion cub whose father was king of the Pride Lands. Someday Simba would be king, too. Mufasa explained that it was all a part of the circle of life.

For now, Simba loved to play with his friend Nala and hang out with his dad. Nala was his best friend. Mufasa was his hero.

"Look, Simba. Everything the light touches is our kingdom," the Lion King told his son. "A king's time as ruler rises and falls like the sun. One day, Simba, the sun will set on my time here and will rise with you as the new king."

One day Simba's jealous uncle, Scar, told him about the Elephant Graveyard. Scar knew Simba would be curious, and he was right. Simba could hardly wait to see the forbidden place. He and Nala headed out together, but they quickly ran into trouble. Three hyenas began chasing them. Simba and Nala were in serious danger!

The Lion King, Mufasa, raced to the rescue.

He saved Simba and Nala.

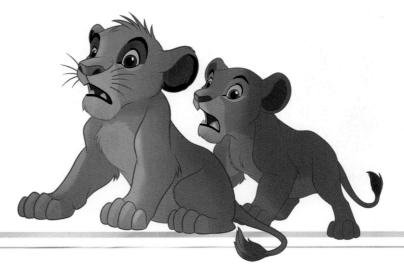

Mufasa was upset with Simba for putting both himself and
Nala in danger. But he soon forgave his son.

That night father and son looked up at the night sky together.
Mufasa explained that his parents and grandparents were up
there, looking down on them both.

He found comfort in the stars.

"Whenever you feel alone, just remember that those kings will
always be there to guide you. And so will I," Mufasa said.

Soon afterward the vicious Scar set up a wildebeest stampede with Simba at its center. It was part of his plot to destroy Mufasa, and it worked.

The brave lion king ran to save his son, and he was killed.

Simba was devastated. He loved his father, and now he was gone. Scar blamed him for Mufasa's passing.

Feeling responsible for his father's death, Simba ran far, far away.

In a jungle oasis, Simba met a meerkat named Timon and a warthog named Pumbaa.

"Gee, he looks blue," Timon said.

"I'd say brownish gold," Pumbaa replied.

"No, no, no, no!" Timon clarified. "I mean he's depressed."

The trio became friends. Timon and Pumbaa helped Simba forget his past. He learned to eat bugs and splash in the water, putting aside his troubles.

Meanwhile, back in the Pride Lands, Scar had taken over Pride Rock. He was a terrible king. The trees and plants were dying out. Many of the animals had left, and the animals who remained were going hungry.

One day Nala, now grown up, arrived at Simba's new home and told him the Pride Lands needed him.

Soon after Nala's visit, Simba looked up into the night sky, the same way he had with his father years ago. He saw his father among the stars.

"You have forgotten who you are, and so have forgotten me," Mufasa said to his son. "Look inside yourself, Simba. You are more than what you have become."

Simba heard his father. And he knew what he had to do.

Simba returned to Pride Rock. He defeated Scar and took his rightful place as Lion King.

Later he and Nala had a cub of their own. One day that cub would also become leader of the Pride Lands. And one day that cub would look up at the stars and see Simba there as a guide.

It was all part of the circle of life.

THE WONDER OF
FAMILY

*"Only an act of true love
can thaw a frozen heart."*
—Grand Pabbie

FROZEN

LONG AGO TWO SISTERS, Princesses Anna and Elsa, lived in the kingdom of Arendelle. They loved each other, and they enjoyed playing together as much as they could.

Their family had a secret: Elsa had a magical power. She could create ice and snow. One night she created a special winter wonderland, where she and Anna played with a little snowman named Olaf. Then Elsa accidentally struck Anna with an icy blast.

The king and queen rushed Anna to a troll named Grand Pabbie. He saved Anna by erasing her memories of Elsa's magic.

The king and queen helped Elsa hide her magic by giving her gloves. They closed the gates to the castle and became isolated.

Years later, when the king and queen were lost at sea, the sisters became even lonelier.

Finally, the time came for Elsa to become queen. On her coronation day, she was nervous about seeing people. Her emotions often made her magic appear, and she did not know how to control it.

Meanwhile, Anna was excited about seeing people arrive for the celebration. She even met and fell in love with the handsome Prince Hans.

At the celebration ball, Anna and Prince Hans happily went to Elsa to tell her that they wanted to get married. But Elsa, now queen, refused to bless the marriage.

Anna was upset. For years she had felt alone. Now Elsa was trying to block her marriage to Hans!

"Why do you shut me out?" she said to Elsa. "What are you so afraid of?"

Worried about Anna marrying the first man she met, and filled with emotion, Elsa lost control of her magic. Ice shot from her hands, cascading around the palace. Panicking, Elsa ran outside. Everywhere she stepped and everything she touched was freezing.

Now that everyone knew her secret, Queen Elsa fled across the harbor, freezing the waters there, and then raced up into the mountains. At the top of the North Mountain, she finally let her magic loose and created her own palace of ice.

Anna felt terrible. She wanted to find her sister, and she
wanted her sister's help to bring summer back to their kingdom.
Leaving Hans in charge of the kingdom, Anna went up into
the mountains to seek out Elsa. There she met an ice harvester
named Kristoff and his reindeer, Sven. They became her guides.

As they climbed higher and higher, they encountered even
more ice and snow. Soon they met a talking snowman.

"Hi, I'm Olaf," he said. The friendly snowman was
happy to lead them to Elsa.

Once inside Elsa's new home, Anna begged her sister to bring summer back to Arendelle.

"You can just unfreeze it," Anna suggested.

This frustrated Elsa. She didn't know how to unfreeze her kingdom. Now that her powers were unleashed, she didn't know how to stop them.

"I can't!" she exclaimed.

With that, an icy blast shot across the room. It was an accident. Elsa didn't even see the ice hit Anna in the heart.

Kristoff tried to help Anna. He rushed her to Grand Pabbie. Grand Pabbie said the ice was making Anna's heart freeze.

"Only an act of true love can thaw a frozen heart," he said.

So Anna, Kristoff, Sven, and Olaf raced back to Arendelle to find Hans. Maybe he could heal her.

Down in Arendelle, Hans got a group of men together. The kingdom was freezing, and he needed to find Elsa to try to stop the suffering.

Together they climbed the icy cold mountain. Several men found Elsa. They shot at her with their crossbows. The queen defended herself by forming walls of ice as shields.

When Hans arrived, he called out, "Queen Elsa!" He begged, "Don't be the monster they fear you are!"

For a moment, Elsa trusted Hans. Then one of the men aimed his crossbow at her. Hans deflected it from Elsa, but the arrow hit an icy chandelier. Elsa ran to escape as the chandelier began to fall toward her, but she slipped and was knocked unconscious.

When she awoke, Elsa found herself imprisoned in the dungeon of her old castle in Arendelle. Hans had tricked her and put her there. He had also refused to kiss Anna to save her life and instead left her in a locked room to freeze with her icy heart.

Elsa managed to escape from her cell. And with a little help from Olaf, Anna escaped, too!

Out in the storm, Hans found Elsa. He raised his sword. Anna rushed to her sister. She was able to block the blow, but her heart finally froze and she turned completely to ice.

Anna had saved Elsa. And that was the act of true love that both sisters needed. As Anna began to thaw, Elsa hugged her. The two sisters wept with joy.

"An act of true love will thaw a frozen heart," Olaf said with a happy sigh.

Drawing now upon love and not fear, Elsa was able to stop the eternal winter and bring summer back. They also shipped Hans to his home far, far away from Arendelle.

And so the two sisters once again shared their lives and happy times together—and did so forever (with Olaf and Kristoff and Sven, too!).

THE WONDER OF
FAMILY

*"There is nowhere you could
go that I won't be with you."*
—Gramma Tala

MOANA

MOANA WAS THE DAUGHTER

of the chief of Motunui. She loved her family. Even when she went on great adventures, she found her way back home.

"There is nowhere you could go that I won't be with you," her grandmother Tala had once said to her.

But today Moana was just going to another part of the island in search of sugarcane. She was helping some of her friends in the village as they prepared a feast for everyone to share.

"May we come, too?" asked a girl named Fetuao. "We love exploring."

She and her friends Laumei, Masina, and Toa were excited to go.

"Yes, but we all have to stick together," Moana said, happy to have the company. "The island is big, and I don't want anyone to get lost."

"Oh, good!" Toa said. He loved sugarcane.

"Great!" Moana said. "Just follow me! I'm looking for a new path to the sugarcane—a shortcut."

Even as they searched for the shortcut, it was still a long hike. Moana was feeling a little lost. After a while, they came across some coconut trees.

"May we stop for a snack?" asked Laumei.

Moana quickly agreed. It was nice to drink the cool coconut milk and eat the coconut meat.

"Now may we play hide-and-seek?" asked Fetuao.

"That sounds fun," Moana said. "But remember: if you get lost, just stay where you are, and I will find you."

"Look!" Toa shouted. "Look at that bird!"

"That's pretty!" Moana said. Then she laughed. "And who knows—maybe it can show us the shortcut to the sugarcane."

That intrigued Toa. Meanwhile, Moana closed her eyes and was counting to ten. Everyone found a terrific hiding spot—everyone, that is, except Toa. Instead of hiding, he kept following the orange-and-blue bird. Fascinated, he followed it deep into the trees.

After a while, Toa realized he was lost. He was scared for a few minutes, but then he remembered what Moana had told them: *If you get lost, just stay where you are, and I will find you.*

Toa sat down next to the bird in its nest. Then he waited . . . and waited . . . and waited.

He was glad to have the bird as company. Its pretty colors and happy song kept him from getting lonely or scared.

"There you are!" Moana said at last. As soon as she had realized Toa was lost, she had thought of the bird. She had found Toa by following some feathers the bird had left.

"I thought the bird might lead us to the shortcut," Toa said. "I'm sorry."

"That's because I was being silly. I said it might lead us to the shortcut because I was a little lost," Moana said. "I'm just glad I found you."

Toa pointed up at a tree. "The bird found her family, too."

"That's what family does," Moana said.

Not far beyond the bird's nest, Moana found a lookout. And from the lookout, she saw the sugarcane field!

"Well, I guess that bird did show us the shortcut after all," she said.

"Yay!" the children cheered.

They ran down to the fields and cut just enough sugarcane to help with the feast that night. Then they returned home, taking the best shortcut ever.

THE WONDER OF
FAMILY

"Your dad's been fighting the entire ocean looking for you."

—Nigel

FINDING
NEMO

NEMO WAS A LITTLE clownfish. He lived with his father, Marlin, on the Great Barrier Reef. Nemo longed for adventure. But Marlin always worried. He worried about big fish who might hurt Nemo, and he worried because Nemo had been born with a lucky fin. Nemo's right fin was smaller than his left fin.

On the first day of school, Marlin took Nemo to class. Nemo's teacher, Mr. Ray, promised Marlin that Nemo would be safe.

But when Marlin found out that the class was going to the Drop-off, Marlin chased after his son.

At the Drop-off, Nemo and his new friends dared one another to swim out and touch a dive boat. Marlin tried to stop him, but Nemo still swam out on the dare. Elated, he reached out and touched the boat. But as he started to swim back, a diver appeared and caught him!

Marlin watched in terror. He raced out and tried to rescue his son, but he wasn't fast enough.

Marlin swam as hard as he could after Nemo, but the diver in the boat was too fast. As the diver sped off, his mask dropped into the sea.

Soon Marlin met a fish named Dory.

"I have to find the boat!" Marlin explained.

Dory had just seen the boat! She quickly led the way toward the boat. After a while, Dory stopped. She glared at Marlin, wanting to know why he was following her. Confused, Marlin explained that she was leading him toward the boat.

"Ohhh, no." Dory sighed apologetically. "I have short-term memory loss," she explained. "I forget things almost instantly."

Still, she wanted to help. Together, Marlin and Dory tried to get the diver's mask. It had writing on it, and Marlin thought it might help him find Nemo. Along the way, they met some sharks who wanted to eat them. Luckily, they escaped . . . and kept looking for Nemo.

Miles away, Nemo found himself in a fish tank at a dentist's office. The other fish in the tank called themselves the Tank Gang. They had a big plan to escape. If someone jammed the filter, the dentist would have to take the fish out of the tank to clean it. They could escape by rolling out the window and into the harbor. It was a good plan. Nemo even tried to help!

But escaping was not so easy.

The plan did not work, and Nemo nearly got sucked into the filter.

"Help me!" Nemo called out. The Tank Gang worked together to pull him to safety, but it was scary for the little clownfish.

Back in the ocean, Dory and Marlin had escaped the sharks and dragged the mask into a deep, dark cave. Marlin tried to distract a giant anglerfish while Dory studied the writing on the mask.

"I can't see," Dory complained.

"Just read it!" Marlin screamed as he desperately tried to keep the anglerfish from eating them both.

"'P. Sherman, 42 Wallaby Way, Sydney,'" Dory read.

"We did it!" Marlin exclaimed. He knew that must be the address where he could finally find Nemo.

Lots of sea creatures heard the story about Marlin trying to find his son, Nemo. A pelican named Nigel flew to the window of the dentist's office.

"Your dad's been fighting the entire ocean looking for you," he told Nemo.

"Really?" Nemo asked. His dad was risking everything to save him!

Nigel explained that Marlin had taken on sharks and jellyfish to find Nemo.

Nemo exclaimed, "He took on a shark!"

Nemo wanted to see his dad again, too. But how? The Tank Gang's first escape plan to jam the filter with a pebble had failed.

But now Nemo had another idea. The dentist wanted to give Nemo to his niece, Darla, on her next visit. When he put Nemo in a plastic bag, Nemo played dead. He was dropped into a drain and—*SWOOSH!*—out into the harbor. That was where Dory found him. And so did his dad.

"Nemo? NEMO?" Marlin called out.

"Daddy! Daaaad!" Nemo cried.

Father and son hugged long and tightly. "It's all right, Son," Marlin said. "It's gonna be okay."

Several weeks later, Nemo was back home and ready for school again. Marlin was there, along with a lot of Marlin's new friends from the ocean.

Nemo waved as he swam away.

"Bye, Dad!" he called out. "Oh, wait! I forgot something." He swam back and hugged Marlin.

"Love you, Dad."

"I love you, too, Son."

Nemo happily swam off to join Mr. Ray and the rest of the class. Marlin watched him go, this time feeling that his beloved son would be okay.

THE WONDER OF
FRIENDSHIP

"I made a good choice."
"In what?"
"My best friend."
—Mater and Lightning

CARS

IT WAS THE DAY of the biggest race of the year. Hotshot rookie Lightning McQueen wanted to win. But instead of winning, Lightning had a tough race. He didn't take any advice from his crew. While he was waiting for the final results, a reporter asked, "Are you sorry you didn't have a crew chief out there?"

"No," said Lightning. "I'm a one-man show."

Just then an announcement came over the loudspeaker: "A tiebreaker race will be held in California in one week."

Lightning took his one-man show on the road toward California. But while he was asleep, he accidentally fell out of the back of his truck and spun out of control.

When he woke up, Lightning was careening down the wrong side of a highway!

He was completely lost. Panicking, he caught his tires on some wires, causing all kinds of damage to the road. That was when Sheriff pulled him over in the little town of Radiator Springs.

"You're in a heap of trouble," Sheriff said to Lightning as he locked him up for the night.

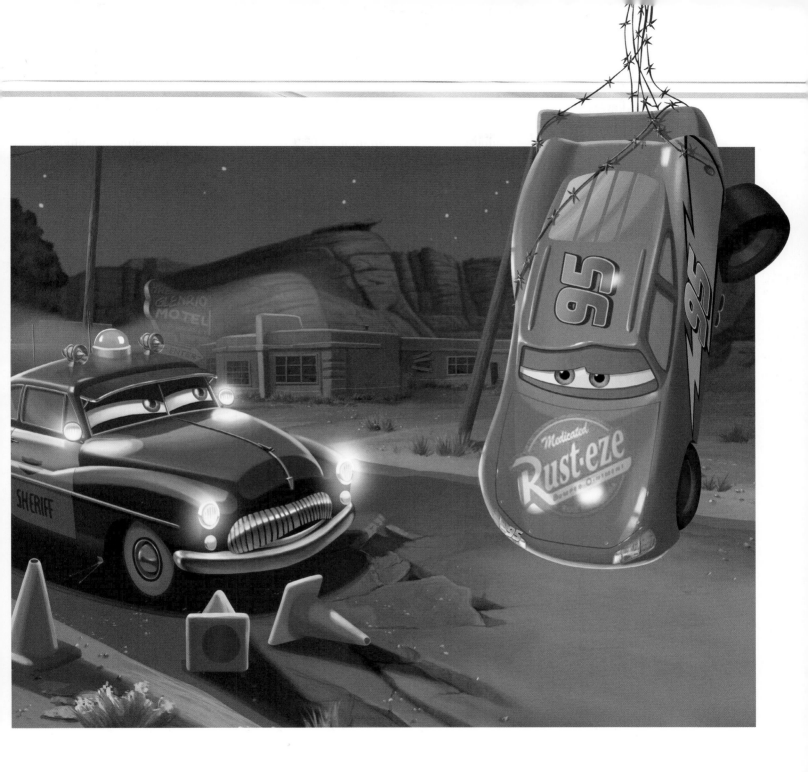

The next morning, Lightning woke up with a parking boot on one of his tires. He felt alone and confused.

He looked around. All the flashy race car could see was a rusty old tow truck with a missing headlight. Lightning scowled as the tow truck introduced himself.

"My name's Mater," the tow truck said.

"Mater?" Lightning said.

"Yeah, like *tuh-mater* but without the *tuh*."

Soon Sheriff showed up and scolded Mater.

"Quit your yapping and tow this delinquent road hazard to traffic court!" he demanded.

The judge was a gruff blue car named Doc Hudson. He was angry that Lightning had ruined their main street. He ordered Lightning to stay in Radiator Springs and repair the pavement.

But Lightning was in a rush. He wanted to get out of town and get to his big race. Instead of fixing the road, he made a big mess.

All the other cars in town were disappointed, but Doc was angry. He told Lightning to keep working.

"I'm not a bulldozer," Lightning said to Doc. "I'm a race car."

Lightning didn't know it, but Doc was an old racing legend himself. He challenged Lightning to a race. "If you win, you go. If I win, you do the road my way," he said.

Lightning quickly agreed. But when he tried to race on an old dirt road, he spun right over a cliff.

"You drive like you fix roads!" Doc hollered down at Lightning. "Lousy!"

He told Mater to haul Lightning up from the cacti.

"I was starting to think he knowed you was gonna crash," Mater said to the grumpy race car.

Lightning was furious, but he got back to work. And **Mater kept encouraging him.** The next morning, the cars of Radiator Springs awoke to the sound of Mater cheering. He was driving circles on a section of smooth, newly paved road.

Lightning had done such a good job that even Doc was impressed. Later, on the dirt road outside of town, he gave the rookie some advice: turn right to go left. It worked. Lightning appreciated the advice. And he appreciated Doc.

No more one-man show!

Lightning was starting to form some friendships, but the biggest bond was with Mater, who kept encouraging him.

That night, Mater invited Lightning to go tractor-tipping. It was scary and fun. When they got back to town, the two felt like best buddies.

"I knew it," Mater said. "I made a good choice."

"In what?" Lightning asked.

"My best friend," answered Mater.

The hotshot rookie smiled. He needed a good friend, and he was glad that it was Mater.

THE WONDER OF
FRIENDSHIP

"That's what friends do!"
—Thumper

BAMBI

IT WAS A LOVELY spring day, and the forest was buzzing with excitement. The birds began chirping the news. Chipmunks chattered in delight. Skunks and mice and even raccoons came out of their dens to race toward a little glade not far from where they lived.

A little bunny named Thumper was among them. He stopped in front of a hole above him in a large tree.

"Wake up, Friend Owl!" Thumper called out. "The new prince is born!"

Thumper was among the first to meet the new young prince. His name was Bambi, and he was just a little fawn who still had white spots on his back.

Thumper was also there when Bambi tried to take his first steps. The little deer stood up and fell right down again.

Kerplunk!

"He doesn't walk very good, does he?" Thumper said.

He thought the little guy needed some encouragement. Then Thumper got an idea. He would be Bambi's very good friend.

For starters, Thumper began encouraging Bambi to try again.

That's what friends do! Thumper thought.

Thumper's siblings helped out, too.

"Get up!" they cried. "Try again!"

They all cheered on the young prince as he struggled to stand.
Thumper encouraged Bambi as he wobbled and almost fell again.
It was hard work, but soon Bambi succeeded.

From then on, Bambi and Thumper were the best of friends.

Thumper began to show Bambi all around the forest.

He showed him lots of new things. He even introduced him to some new friends.

When a butterfly landed on Bambi's tail, Bambi looked delighted. The butterfly tickled Bambi, and the young deer giggled.

Thumper laughed out loud. He liked introducing Bambi to all the wonderful things around him.

"That's what friends do!" Thumper explained to his friend.

Thumper soon realized that Bambi liked exploring a lot. Thumper did, too!

So they explored more together.

"That's what friends do!" Thumper said.

He showed Bambi some flowers.

"Flower," Thumper said, teaching his friend a new word. Bambi began to sniff the flowers and came nose to nose with a little skunk!

"Flower!" Bambi said proudly. Thumper laughed. The skunk laughed. Now all three were friends, and the little skunk went by a new name: Flower!

Thumper and Bambi continued playing and laughing and exploring together all spring. Thumper taught Bambi more new words. He showed him fun places to run and play. They went on lots of new adventures together, too.

"That's what friends do!" Thumper said. "They find lots of new stuff, they meet new friends, and they play a whole bunch."

Bambi smiled and knew this was true. A friend was a friend, and now both Thumper and Bambi knew they would be friends for a very long time.

THE WONDER OF
FRIENDSHIP

"Over in that house is a kid who thinks you are the greatest. And it's not because you're a space ranger. It's because you're a toy. You are his toy."

—*Woody*

TOY STORY

WOODY WAS ANDY'S FAVORITE toy. They were best friends!

One day a new toy arrived in Andy's room. His name was Buzz Lightyear. He thought he was a real space ranger, not a toy.

"To infinity and beyond!" Buzz said.

Andy loved him. He played with Buzz all the time.

Woody started to feel left out. He was sad.

Didn't Andy love him anymore?

Andy's family was getting ready to move. That night they were going to Pizza Planet for dinner. Andy was allowed to take one toy with him. Woody wanted to be that one toy. He tried to push Buzz out of the way so Andy wouldn't see him. Instead, Woody accidentally pushed Buzz out the window!

The other toys in Andy's room gasped. They thought of Woody as their leader. He was their friend! But this was not a friendly thing to do.

Andy ended up taking Woody to Pizza Planet. But as their car pulled out of the driveway, Buzz ran out of the bushes and chased them!

After a wild car ride, Woody and Buzz got separated from Andy's family! Eventually they worked together and found Andy again at Pizza Planet.

Unfortunately, something else caught Buzz's eye: the Spaceship Crane Game. Buzz still thought he was a real space ranger. He raced over to the game, thinking the spaceship was his real ship.

Woody ran to stop him. He didn't want Buzz to get captured. He was starting to think of Buzz as a friend.

Unfortunately, Woody was too late to save his new buddy.

Andy's neighbor Sid, the kid who was no friend to his toys, ended up capturing Buzz.

As Buzz was lifted up, up, up . . . Woody clung to his leg. He was trying to help!

Sadly, Sid captured both toys and took them home.

Sid had lots of broken toys at his house. Buzz and Woody were scared!

They wanted to escape and return to Andy's house next door. When they saw Sid's dog, Scud, they ran and got separated. As Buzz ducked through an open door, he saw a TV ad. It was for the Buzz Lightyear toy.

"Is it true?" Buzz gasped. "Am I really . . . a toy?"

Buzz was crushed. He'd thought he was a real space ranger.

A little while later, Sid tied a rocket to Buzz. He wanted to launch the ranger into space. Buzz was too sad to care.

Woody could see that Buzz was down and out. He could see he needed help!

He tried to free his friend from the rocket, but he couldn't.

"You were right," Buzz said sadly. "I'm just a toy."

Woody tried to cheer him up by pointing at Andy's room next door. "Over in that house is a kid who thinks you are the greatest," he said. "And it's not because you're a space ranger. It's because you're a toy. You are his toy."

The next morning, Woody helped Buzz escape through Sid's fence. Then both toys raced after Andy's moving van. The other toys from Andy's room tried to help them. They finally saw that Woody was helping Buzz.

The two toys were friends!

Woody might have accidentally knocked Buzz out the window before, but now he was doing everything to rescue him.

Unfortunately, it was all too much. They couldn't quite get onto the fast-moving truck.

Then Buzz got an idea.

"Woody!" Buzz yelled to his friend. "The rocket!"

Woody lit the fuse, and they flew into the sky.
What a team!

Seconds later they dropped gently through the sunroof of Andy's car in front of the moving van. Woody and Buzz were back where they belonged—with Andy. Their adventure was over, but their friendship was just beginning.

THE WONDER OF
KINDNESS

"One bite and all your
dreams will come true!"
—the Queen

SNOW
WHITE

ONCE UPON A TIME, Snow White lived with her stepmother, the Queen. Snow White loved spending time with her animal friends. One afternoon while she was singing with some doves at the wishing well, a prince heard her. The kind young man joined her in song. Snow White fell in love with his singing voice immediately.

One day the Queen looked into her Magic Mirror.

It told her that Snow White was more beautiful than she was. The Queen was instantly enraged.

Once she heard of the Queen's anger, Snow White knew she was in danger and fled into the forest.

But the forest seemed different in the dark of night, and Snow White was scared. She ran until she collapsed, sobbing.

As she cried, dawn began to break. Some animals crept out to comfort her as she hid her head in her arms.

A little bird lit on her finger. Slowly Snow White looked up. She could see that the animals were friendly. They reminded her of her animal friends at the castle. They were kind to her, and she started to feel better.

Together they wandered through the woods until they found a small clearing.

The sun sparkled down on a friendly-looking cottage.

With her new friends by her side, Snow White carefully crossed a little brook and entered the glade. The deer and the bunnies went right up to the front of the cottage. Snow White followed them and wiped a bit of dust off the windows so she could peer inside. Nobody seemed to be home.

It looked warm and inviting, not at all like the dark and scary forest where Snow White had spent the night.

"Hello?" Snow White called out as she opened the door. "May I come in?"

But nobody was inside. A bunny and a chipmunk scampered past and began to sniff the floor. It seemed safe enough. And the little cottage was so welcoming that Snow White immediately felt at home.

She looked about and found seven little chairs at the table. She saw dishes piled high in the sink and clothes strewn about. Then she found seven little beds with seven names on the footboards.

Exhausted after her long night in the woods, Snow White fell asleep.

Later she awoke to a sound and saw seven little people come into the room.

At first the men weren't sure what to make of Snow White.

Snow White smiled. She looked at their names on the beds and tried to guess who was who. She figured out who Grumpy was right away.

Then Snow White told them her story.

"She won't find me here," she said of the Queen.

Later they all ate supper together and played music.

Unfortunately, the Queen did find Snow White. She disguised herself and went into the forest to find the princess. While her new friends were out working in their diamond mine, Snow White was all alone. The disguised Queen arrived at the cottage and offered Snow White a poisoned apple.

"It's a magic wishing apple," the Queen said.

"A wishing apple?" Snow White replied, filled with curiosity.

"One bite and all your dreams will come true!"

Snow White could not resist. She took a bite and fell into a deep sleep.

Snow White's animal friends ran to the men in the diamond mine, and they all ran back to the cottage. As soon as the Queen saw them, she hurried away, never to be heard from again.

Still, Snow White would not awake. With sadness in their hearts, the men finally laid her on a bed of roses and wept.

Then something magical happened. The Prince, who had sung with Snow White at the wishing well, discovered her in the woods. He loved her truly, and that was enough to break the spell.

Snow White awoke. The men cheered. Her animal friends danced with joy. And the Prince and Snow White found true happiness together.

THE WONDER OF
KINDNESS

*"You can't go to the
ball looking like that!"*
—the Fairy Godmother

CINDERELLA

CINDERELLA LIVED IN AN old château with her unkind stepmother, Lady Tremaine, and her stepsisters. Still she managed to be happy in her home. She always treated her animal friends with kindness and love, and they loved her in return.

One day, the king sent out an invitation to a royal ball. He invited everyone in the kingdom.

Of course, Lady Tremaine wanted to keep Cinderella from going. "Well," she said, "I see no reason why you can't go . . . if you get all your work done. And if you can find something suitable to wear."

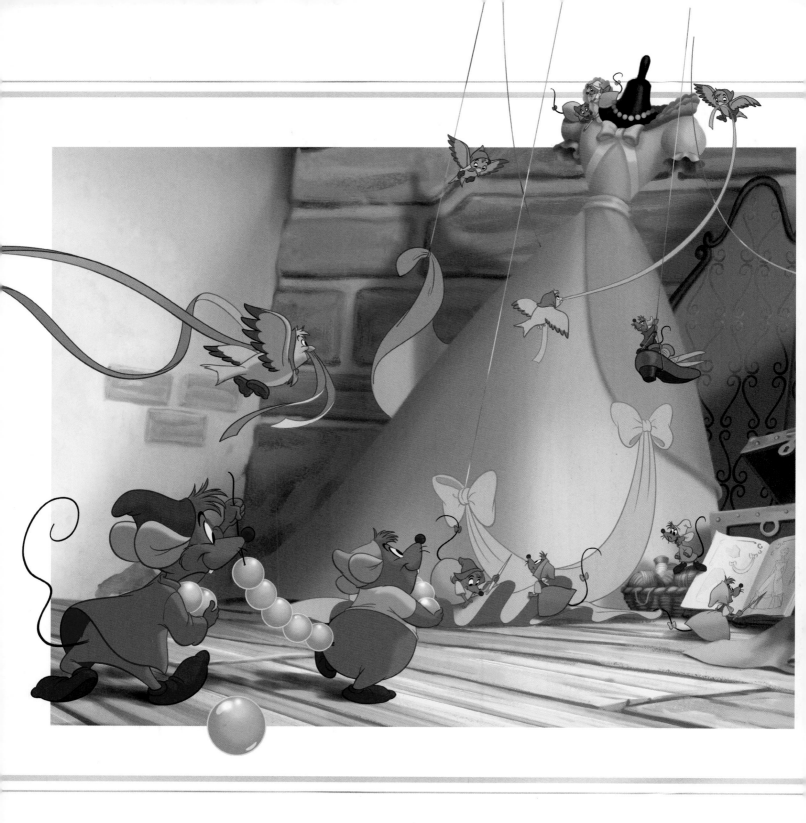

Cinderella's animal friends wanted to help her.

They knew Cinderella did not have a ball gown, so they decided to fix an old dress that had belonged to her mother.

The kind animals mended the dress. Soon it looked like new!

When Cinderella finished her work and saw the dress, she was delighted.

But her stepsisters were jealous. They tore apart the dress, leaving Cinderella heartbroken. How could she go to the ball with no dress and no way to get there?

Cinderella had just about lost hope when, quite magically, her fairy godmother appeared.

The Fairy Godmother looked around at the old barnyard and said: "I'd say the first thing you need is a pumpkin."

And with a wave of her magic wand and a few magical words— *POOF!*—she transformed the pumpkin into a sparkling coach.

Then, looking at Cinderella's beloved animal friends, she transformed them into a horse, a coachman, and elegant footmen.

Then the Fairy Godmother exclaimed, "You can't go to the ball looking like that!"

Once again, she waved her magic wand, and this time she created a gown.

"Oh, it's a beautiful dress!" Cinderella exclaimed. "Why, it's like a dream! A wonderful dream come true!"

"But like all dreams, I'm afraid this can't last forever," the Fairy Godmother warned Cinderella kindly. "On the stroke of twelve, the spell will be broken, and everything will be as it was before."

Cinderella and her friends rode to the palace, and she entered the ballroom. Everyone turned to look at the beautiful young lady. Who was she? They didn't remember seeing her before!

The Prince went right up to Cinderella and introduced himself. They danced, and they talked late into the night. They had a lot in common, and they both were falling in love. It was a wonderful night.

As the clock began to strike twelve, Cinderella remembered what her fairy godmother had said. The spell would soon be broken.

She ran from the palace as her gown and pumpkin coach transformed back to their old selves.

The next day, Lady Tremaine locked Cinderella in her room. She knew that Cinderella and the Prince had met the night before. She was angry that the Prince liked Cinderella more than he liked her own daughters.

But Cinderella's kind and loving mouse friends risked everything to help her escape.

Meanwhile, the Prince had been hoping to find her again. As Cinderella had run from the ball, she had left behind one of her glass slippers. The Prince had picked it up, hoping to find the lovely woman whose foot fit that slipper. And he did.

Cinderella's mouse friends all cheered in delight. Her bird friends chirped and fluttered their wings. They simply knew that their favorite person had found her perfect match.

The Prince and Cinderella were indeed in love. They married and lived happily ever after.

And as for Cinderella's animal friends, they lived happily ever after, too, always devoted to their loving and kind friend, Cinderella.

THE WONDER OF
KINDNESS

"You came back."
—the Beast

BEAUTY
AND THE
BEAST

BELLE LIVED IN A small village with her father, Maurice. She spent much of her days reading about faraway places. The villagers thought it odd to see such a young, beautiful girl with her nose in a book all the time.

Maurice was an inventor. He was brilliant and creative . . . but a bit absentminded. One day he left for a fair to display his latest invention. Unfortunately, he was caught in a terrible storm. He found shelter in a large and frightening old castle.

When his horse returned home without him, Belle raced to see if she could find her father. The horse led Belle right up to the castle. Though it was frightening, Belle ventured inside.

The castle belonged to a terrifying beast.

Once upon a time, the Beast had been a prince. When he had cruelly turned away an enchantress seeking shelter, she had cast a spell. All the Prince's servants were turned into enchanted objects. The Prince himself was turned into the Beast. The spell could be broken only if the Prince learned to love and be loved in return.

Now the Beast held Belle's father as prisoner. Belle begged the Beast to set her father free. In return, she would stay at the castle.

"You would take his place?" the Beast asked, astonished. Reluctantly he agreed.

Later that night, the enchanted objects decided to welcome Belle. They led Belle downstairs, where they entertained her.

After dinner, Belle explored the castle and soon found herself in the forbidden West Wing. There she discovered a single rose in a glass jar. It was the enchanted rose left behind by the Enchantress years earlier. If the spell was not broken before the last petal fell from the rose, then it would never be broken. The Beast and all the enchanted objects would remain forever in their current states.

Belle did not know that. When she felt a shadow fall over her, she turned and saw the Beast.

"Get out!" he shouted. He told her to stay away from the West Wing . . . and the enchanted rose. Terrified, she fled.

Belle escaped into the forest, where she soon found herself in danger. She was surprised when the Beast came to her rescue. However, he was hurt in the process.

Belle could not abandon him. She took him back to the castle and treated his injuries. She was grateful to the Beast for saving her, but she told him he needed to control his temper—and he knew she was right.

Belle began to spend time with the Beast. They dined together, they explored books together in the castle library, and they went on walks together.

Belle began to see kindness in the Beast. And he saw the same in her.

Though they did not realize it fully, the Beast and Belle were becoming friends.

Still Belle worried about her father. She wanted to go see him. The Beast sadly agreed to let her go. He had begun to love her. And even though he and the enchanted objects knew that this love could break the spell, the Beast also knew that Belle needed to be free.

She returned to the village and her father.

Not long afterward, the villagers attacked the castle. They were scared of the Beast, and they wanted to hurt him.

But when they nearly killed him, Belle ran to him.

"Belle," the Beast whispered. "You came back."

"Please don't leave me," Belle told the dying Beast. "I love you."

And with that, the spell was broken. The Beast loved and was loved in return. He and the enchanted objects became human again.

Belle looked closely at the Prince. Was he the one she had grown to love?

"It is you!" she said, recognizing him at last.

And they all lived happily ever after.

THE WONDER OF
ADVENTURE

"Thanks for the adventure.
Now go have a new one."
—Ellie

AS A LITTLE KID, Carl Fredricksen wanted to be an explorer. His hero was the legendary explorer Charles F. Muntz.

"Adventure is out there!" Muntz liked to say.

One day, Carl's best friend, Ellie, showed him her adventure book. Inside was a picture of Paradise Falls in South America.

When Carl and Ellie grew up, they got married. Carl sold balloons from a cart, and Ellie took care of animals at the zoo. They were very happy. They had lots of little adventures at home. But they never got all the way to Paradise Falls.

After Ellie died, Carl lived alone. He felt lost and sad. One day, Carl got news that he would have to leave his beloved house and move. Remembering his old promises to Ellie to find adventure, he made a plan. He was a balloon guy, after all! So he tied thousands of balloons to his house and set sail for Paradise Falls.

Up, up, up went the house!

Suddenly he heard something on his porch. It was Russell, a Junior Wilderness Explorer. He'd been hoping to get his Assisting the Elderly badge. Now both of them were on the adventure of a lifetime.

Soon the little house flew into a storm. Carl and Russell were swept all the way to South America.

They landed just a few miles from Paradise Falls!

Carl and Russell made harnesses out of garden hoses and pulled his floating house behind them as they walked toward the falls and their great adventure.

Carl looked all around him. Everything was exactly as he and Ellie had imagined. He knew she would have loved it there.

Soon they met a giant bird. Russell liked the bird right away. He wanted to be friends. He named the bird Kevin.

Kevin liked chocolate, so Russell left a trail of chocolate for the bird to follow. They became a team of adventurers!

Russell loved Kevin so much! They had lots of fun together.

It turned out Kevin was a mother! She had babies at home. Of course, Russell and Carl now had to protect her and help her get home to her babies.

Then they met a talking dog named Dug.

"My name is Dug. I have just met you, and I love you," Dug said.

The dog was easily distracted. "Squirrel!" he called out every time he saw one—even in midsentence.

But things started to get complicated. Dug had been sent on a mission to find the bird.

Luckily, Dug was so friendly that he also began to like Kevin a lot.

The next day four fierce dogs from Dug's pack burst out of the bushes! They were looking for Kevin, too. The dogs led Carl and Russell to Charles F. Muntz, Carl's long-lost childhood hero! Muntz told Carl and Russell about his search for the Monster of Paradise Falls.

Carl quickly realized that the "monster" was Kevin. That didn't make any sense. Kevin was a nice bird.

Still, Muntz wanted the bird, and he thought Carl had her.

"Get them!" Muntz called out to his dogs.

Suddenly, Kevin swooped in. The brave bird rescued Carl, Dug, and Russell!

Muntz tracked down the explorers, captured Kevin, and set Carl's house on fire.

Russell and Carl both felt terrible. Carl managed to put out the fire. Then he sat down inside the house and found Ellie's adventure book. He saw a handwritten message from Ellie: "Thanks for the adventure. Now go have a new one."

Carl smiled. Their life together had been an adventure.

Ellie had gotten her wish after all.

Together Russell and Carl found a way to rescue Kevin from the terrible Muntz. Dug helped, too. Carl had to give up his house, but it was worth it. Besides, he still had the memories . . . and some wonderful new memories, too, with his new friends.

When they finally returned home, Carl proudly attended the ceremony where Russell got his Assisting the Elderly badge.

"Wow!" Russell said, giving him an explorer salute. The two friends had had quite an adventure together. And both knew that there were many more to come.

THE WONDER OF
ADVENTURE

"Ladies do not start fights,
but they can finish them."
—Marie

THE
ARISTOCATS

DUCHESS WAS A WHITE Persian cat with three kittens, Toulouse, Berlioz, and Marie. They lived in Paris with their wealthy human, Madame Bonfamille.

Edgar, her butler, also lived with them. Madame Bonfamille made sure that he always served the finest cream to her cats.

The cats were able to practice their arts in Madame's house. Toulouse was a painter. Berlioz played the piano. And Marie liked to sing.

One afternoon before practicing her scales and arpeggios, Marie tumbled with her brothers.

"Ladies do not start fights, but they can finish them," Marie said. Then she announced to her brother, "I'm ready, Maestro."

Berlioz did a fancy move while playing the piano, and it crinkled Marie's tail.

"Oh!" Marie cried. "Mama, he did it again!"

The kittens started their music playing while Duchess watched attentively. She was quite proud of all her kittens and their various talents.

And, of course, Madame adored them to the point of spoiling her dear cats.

Now, this bothered Edgar. One day, after hearing that Madame would leave her vast fortune to the cats instead of him, he became filled with jealousy. How could Madame do such a thing to him when he had been a wonderful butler to her all these years?

"Those cats have got to go," Edgar muttered to himself.

That evening, he put some sleeping powder in the cats' cream and waited for them to fall asleep. Then he took them far into the countryside to get rid of them for good.

Luckily, a country hound chased Edgar. He drove off the road and into a stream. Meanwhile, the cats' basket flew to safety on the shore.

When the cats awoke, they knew they had to get back to Paris and Madame Bonfamille. But how? Luckily, an orange cat named Thomas O'Malley found them.

After Duchess asked O'Malley for help, the orange cat quickly agreed to show the Aristocats the way back to Paris. It was a long, tough journey.

Once, when they were all running from a train, Marie fell off a bridge! She splashed into the water far below. O'Malley jumped in to rescue her while Duchess ran along the shoreline.

Together, they got Marie to safety.

O'Malley led them all the way to their home in Paris. It was time for him to go home while Duchess and the kittens returned to their fancy life in the mansion.

"I'll never forget you, Thomas O'Malley," Duchess said.

Madame Bonfamille was delighted to see her cats home, safe and sound. Edgar, on the other hand, was not. The butler soon caught the cats and was going to put them in a trunk. He wanted to ship them to Timbuktu!

Luckily, Duchess called out to a little mouse named Roquefort: "Go get O'Malley! Run!" The little mouse did exactly that, and soon O'Malley raced to the rescue.

O'Malley tried to save his friends, but it was a tough job for one cat. Roquefort helped unlock the trunk. Then O'Malley was able to open it and pull out Duchess and the kittens.

After that, with a bit of a nudge from Madame Bonfamille's horse, Frou Frou, Edgar sailed across the barn and plunked down into the trunk.

Whomp! The trunk's lid closed with Edgar safely tucked inside, and the butler got shipped to Timbuktu for good.

At last, all the cats breathed a sigh of relief.

Duchess realized that she didn't want O'Malley to go back to his own home. She wanted him to stay with her and the kittens . . . and Madame Bonfamille, of course.

O'Malley was delighted to stay.

He adored Duchess and the kittens. And even though he had a hard time adjusting to bow ties and family portraits, O'Malley soon felt right at home. He had to admit that the soft cushions, the extra petting from Madame, and his brand-new family were awfully nice.

Of course, he also liked the fresh cream!

THE WONDER OF
ADVENTURE

"The human world, it's a mess!
Life under the sea is better than
anything they got up there."

—Sebastian

THE
LITTLE
MERMAID

ARIEL, THE LITTLE MERMAID, was curious, and she loved to explore with her best friend, Flounder.

But her father warned her about going to the surface. It was dangerous above the sea, and the king of the undersea wanted his daughter to stay safe.

The adventurous Ariel still peeked above the surface when she could. One night, she caught a glimpse of a human ship. She saw a prince named Eric. He was handsome, and she could see that he was also strong and kind in the way he captained his ship and took care of his dog, Max.

When the ship ran into a terrible storm, Prince Eric did his best to rescue Max. Instead, Eric got tossed into the sea and pulled under the water.

Ariel had to help. The fearless mermaid dived deep to get him to the surface and to the safety of the shore. There she sang to him.

In time she had to return to the sea. She was, after all, a mermaid. But when Eric regained consciousness, he remembered her.

"A girl rescued me. She was singing. She had the most beautiful voice," he said afterward to his friend Grimsby. He wanted to find her. Perhaps he even loved her.

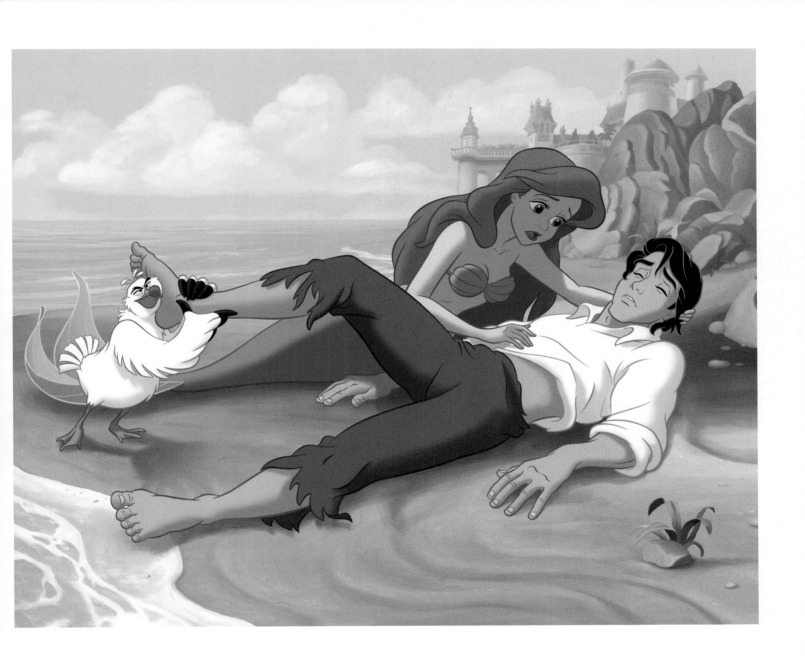

Ariel had felt a strong connection to Eric, too, and she wanted to see him again.

"Ariel, listen to me," her friend Sebastian said. "The human world, it's a mess! Life under the sea is better than anything they got up there."

Then, when Flounder took her to her secret underwater grotto to see a recovered statue of the prince, Ariel was delighted. Unfortunately, her father was not.

"Contact between the human world and the mer-world is strictly forbidden!" King Triton boomed.

King Triton was furious. He destroyed the statue, believing that would somehow keep his daughter safe from the human world.

Ariel was distraught. As she wept, two eels named Flotsam and Jetsam approached and told her to visit the sea witch, Ursula.

So Ariel went to visit the sea witch. Ursula agreed to give Ariel some human legs so she could visit Eric in the human world.

"If he kisses you before the sun sets on the third day, you'll remain human permanently," Ursula said. "But if he doesn't, you turn back into a mermaid, and you belong to me." Ariel agreed to the terms. She longed to be human, and she really wanted to see Eric again.

But Ursula had one more terrible part to her agreement. She wanted to discuss payment.

"What I want from you is your voice," she said. And she took it!

Ariel courageously swam to the surface and tried out her new legs.

Eric was walking on another part of the beach with Max. Max raced over to Ariel as soon as he noticed her.

Eric saw Ariel, too. "You seem very familiar to me. Have we met?" he asked. Ariel nodded. Max barked. The dog recognized her.

"I knew it!" Eric exclaimed. "You're the one—the one I've been looking for!"

But when Ariel could not reply, Eric's heart sank. The woman he loved had had a beautiful singing voice. This could not be the same woman.

Still, Eric wanted to take care of the stranger. He brought her to the castle. There Ariel put on a human dress and learned to walk.

Later Eric took her around the kingdom. One evening, they had a romantic boat ride, and they almost kissed ... because they were truly in love.

But the kiss was interrupted when their boat was tipped over by Ursula's eels, Flotsam and Jetsam.

It turned out that Ursula wanted to prevent that kiss. And she had another trick to keep Ariel from regaining her voice and her freedom. The sea witch disguised herself as a human. With Ariel's voice in a shell around her neck, she was able to convince Eric that she was the woman who had saved him. They arranged for a wedding at sea.

When Ariel understood what had happened, she rushed to the ship. She got her voice back, but a terrible battle ensued. King Triton did all he could to save his daughter. He even allowed Ursula to turn him into a tiny, helpless sea creature while she took over the entire sea. She caused chaos with a massive whirlpool that raised several sunken ships to the surface.

Eric took the helm of one of the ships. He rammed his ship into the sea witch. She sank, never to be heard from again.

The ocean returned to normal, and Triton regained his throne. Seeing how much his daughter loved Eric, King Triton used his magic to make Ariel human.

And so the Little Mermaid began her new adventure with Eric by her side and a song in her heart.

THE WONDER OF
ADVENTURE

"We're not selling the puppies.
Not a single one!"
—*Roger*

101
DALMATIANS

NOT SO VERY LONG ago, two Dalmatians, Pongo and Perdita, lived in a cozy home in London with their two humans, Roger and Anita. They also lived with Nanny, a wonderful cook, housekeeper, and friend.

Perdy was expecting puppies, and the entire household was excited.

Anita's former classmate, Cruella De Vil, came for a visit one day. She had heard about the puppies and also seemed excited. "I live for furs! I worship furs!" Cruella said.

A few weeks afterward, Perdy gave birth.

Just then Cruella appeared in the doorway. "I'll take them all—the whole litter!" she declared.

But Roger refused. "We're not selling the puppies. Not a single one!" he said. "And that's final!"

Unfortunately, Cruella still was obsessed with the puppies. One evening Pongo and Perdy were out on their nightly walk with Roger and Anita. Cruella took the chance to have her two henchmen, Horace and Jasper, steal the puppies. Nanny did her best to stop them, but she simply could not.

Pongo immediately called upon the Twilight Bark.

All the dogs around London began barking to one another. They were sounding the alarm that there had been a puppy-napping!

A cat named Sergeant Tibs and an Old English sheepdog named the Colonel heard the Twilight Bark. They knew just what to do. Following a lead, they found the puppies with Horace and Jasper at the old De Vil place in the country. Not only had Cruella's henchmen taken the fifteen puppies, they also had eighty-four other Dalmatian puppies. It was all part of Cruella's plot to make a spotted fur coat. In all, there were ninety-nine Dalmatian puppies.

The Colonel quickly sent the signal to Pongo and Perdy that he had found their puppies but that they were still in serious trouble.

Horace and Jasper had them locked inside the mansion, and Cruella would soon be back to retrieve them. All ninety-nine puppies needed help—and fast!

Pongo and Perdita ran to the rescue. As soon as they reached the old mansion, they burst through the window. The puppies yipped and yelped to encourage the two adult dogs as they fought off Horace and Jasper and freed the puppies.

Then they took off into the countryside to lead all ninety-nine puppies home. But would they be able to get there safely? Cruella De Vil was still out there, and Horace and Jasper would be looking for the puppies, too.

It was a bitterly cold night when Perdy led the long line of puppies across the snowy fields and roads. Pongo did his best to cover their tracks, but it was hard! The journey was long and difficult, and the poor little puppies were getting hungry and **very, very tired**.

Meanwhile, Cruella De Vil had jumped into her long purple car and was careening around the streets looking for the dogs.

Horace and Jasper were on the trail, too.

"Keep going, keep going!" Pongo urged his brave little puppies.

Finally, Pongo and Perdita found a truck that was big enough to carry the tired puppies. They loaded the puppies into the back, one by one.

And that was when Cruella De Vil spotted them.

"Horace! Jasper!" she called out. "After them!"

The two henchmen followed the truck in a big chase with Cruella following in her car. When they all crashed into each other, the truck carrying the puppies drove off without them. The Dalmatians were safe!

At last Pongo, Perdy, and their fifteen puppies arrived home. The eighty-four other puppies were also there.

They were a little dirty after their adventure, but they were unharmed.

Nanny could hardly believe how many puppies she saw. When she counted them—and included Pongo and Perdita—she gasped and said, "A hundred and one!"

"What will we do with them?" Anita asked.

Roger was quick to answer: "We'll keep them!"

And that is exactly what they did. They moved to the countryside and bought a big house, where the humans and all one hundred and one Dalmatians lived happily for years to come.

THE WONDER OF
COURAGE

*"Look, there's a great big hunk of world
down there with no fence around it, where
two dogs can find adventure and excitement."*
—Tramp

LADY
AND THE
TRAMP

LADY WAS A BELOVED cocker spaniel who was adopted on Christmas by her humans, Jim Dear and Darling. She had two good friends named Jock, a Scottish terrier, and Trusty, a bloodhound.

"Darling is expecting a wee bairn," Jock explained.

"'Bairn'?" Lady asked.

"He means a baby, Miss Lady," said Trusty.

Just then a stray named Tramp walked by. "When a baby moves in," he said, "the dog moves out."

Sure enough, the humans did have a baby. And Lady loved the newborn as much as they did.

Not long after that, Jim Dear and Darling went on a trip. They asked Aunt Sarah to watch the baby while they were gone. Lady also felt responsible for the baby's care.

Unfortunately, Aunt Sarah had two mischievous cats. When they started to go after the family's canary and goldfish, Lady courageously stepped in and stopped them. The cats had made a horrific mess, but Aunt Sarah blamed Lady. She took Lady to the pet store and put a muzzle on her!

Lady was so upset that she ran away.

Lost and confused as she ran in the unfamiliar streets, Lady was grateful when Tramp found her. He took her to meet a beaver friend, who chewed off Lady's muzzle. Afterward, Tramp took Lady to dinner.

Tramp's favorite place to eat was the alley behind Tony's Restaurant. As soon as Tramp arrived with Lady, Tony and his chef, Joe, came out to greet them.

"Hey, Joe!" Tony said. "He says he wants the two-spaghetti special. Heavy on the meatballs!"

Joe served the dinner, and then both men played some romantic music as Tramp and Lady shared their meal—and a kiss!

Lady and Tramp had a wonderful time together. Tramp wanted Lady to stay with him.

"Look, there's a great big hunk of world down there with no fence around it," he said, "where two dogs can find adventure and excitement."

But Lady felt she needed to get home to help with the baby.

Tramp began to walk her home, but he decided to run through a chicken coop first. Minutes later, the dogcatcher came by. Tramp got away, but the dogcatcher caught Lady! He put her in the pound with some stray dogs.

Finally, Aunt Sarah picked up Lady.

The little dog was happy to go home at last. But instead of letting her inside her house, Aunt Sarah tied up Lady outside!

Lady was sad—and also angry with Tramp.

When he showed up to talk with her, she asked him to leave. So that's what he started to do—until Lady spotted a rat climbing up the outside of the house toward the baby's room. Still tied to her post, Lady couldn't stop it.

"A rat!" Lady cried out. "In the baby's room!"

Tramp heard Lady and raced back to help. Bravely he charged into the house. He ran up the stairs, where he cornered the rat and got rid of it.

Tramp was all alone in the baby's room when Aunt Sarah arrived. She called the dogcatcher, and Tramp was taken away.

Just then Jim Dear and Darling returned home. They freed Lady and saw the good that Tramp had done for their baby.

Meanwhile, Jock and Trusty chased down the dogcatcher's truck to rescue Tramp. Trusty was badly hurt, but in the end, everyone was okay. And Tramp was freed.

Jim Dear and Darling adopted Tramp right away. And after all his adventures, Tramp was happy to have a home with a warm and loving family of humans. And at Christmas that year, everyone—*including four brand-new puppies*—celebrated their time together.

THE WONDER OF
COURAGE

"Whee! We did it! We did it!"
—Timothy Q. Mouse

DUMBO

ONE LOVELY EVENING A flock of storks delivered babies to the circus animals. Mrs. Jumbo waited and waited. But it wasn't until the next day that the last stork arrived with a brand-new little elephant.

He was a delightful baby, and even more adorable than Mrs. Jumbo could ever have imagined. She fell in love right away.

The other elephants cooed over him, too. But when the baby elephant sneezed, his ears unfolded. They were enormous! While the other elephants laughed and teased, Mrs. Jumbo tucked baby Dumbo even closer. She adored her little elephant.

The next day Dumbo helped all the elephants raise the big-top tent for the circus. Someday Dumbo would perform inside the tent alongside his mother.

Later there was a big parade. Dumbo proudly marched behind his mother, holding on to her tail. The crowd laughed. Dumbo did not know why. When he arrived back at the circus tent, a mean boy pulled Dumbo's ear and made fun of him.

Dumbo was very sad, and Mrs. Jumbo wanted to protect him. She trumpeted loudly and lifted a bale of hay high over her head. The boy screamed and ran. Just then the Ringmaster arrived. He thought Mrs. Jumbo was acting wild, and he locked her away.

Dumbo and his mother were both distraught. They couldn't see each other.

"Poor little guy," Timothy Q. Mouse said as he watched Dumbo cry. "There he goes—without a friend in the world."

Timothy decided right then and there to become Dumbo's friend. He marched over to the other elephants and told them to be nicer to Dumbo. The elephants were scared of the little mouse!

Then he went to Dumbo and said, "I think your ears are beautiful."

Timothy came up with a plan to make Dumbo a star. He whispered into the Ringmaster's ear while he slept. The next day, the Ringmaster put on an act with all the elephants balancing on a ball. Dumbo would balance at the top!

Timothy tied Dumbo's ears on top of his head. But—oops—the ears came undone. Dumbo tripped and knocked all the other elephants to the ground.

The elephants were angry with Dumbo, so Dumbo started working with the clowns instead. They put him in an act where they pretended to be firefighters putting out a fire in a tower. They placed Dumbo at the top of the tower! But when it was time for Dumbo to jump into a net, he was too afraid.

Poor Dumbo felt terrible. It seemed like he couldn't do any of the circus acts well. But mostly he missed his mother.

Later that night, Timothy led Dumbo to the trailer where Mrs. Jumbo was locked up.

"Mrs. Jumbo!" Timothy called out. "Someone to see you!"

Mrs. Jumbo rushed to the window and reached out her long trunk to caress her baby. She lifted him and rocked him.

Dumbo's tears dried, and he smiled as he swayed in the comfort of his mother's trunk.

The next morning, Timothy and Dumbo woke up in a tree. How had they gotten there?

Suddenly, Timothy put two and two together. He understood how they had ended up in the tree: Dumbo had been able to fly, using his ears! It was his natural gift.

Still, Dumbo was afraid of trying to fly again. So Timothy gave him a magic feather. Dumbo believed in his friend. With his new magic feather tucked into his trunk, Dumbo flew!

"Hot diggity!" Timothy Q. Mouse cried out. "You're flying! You're flying!"

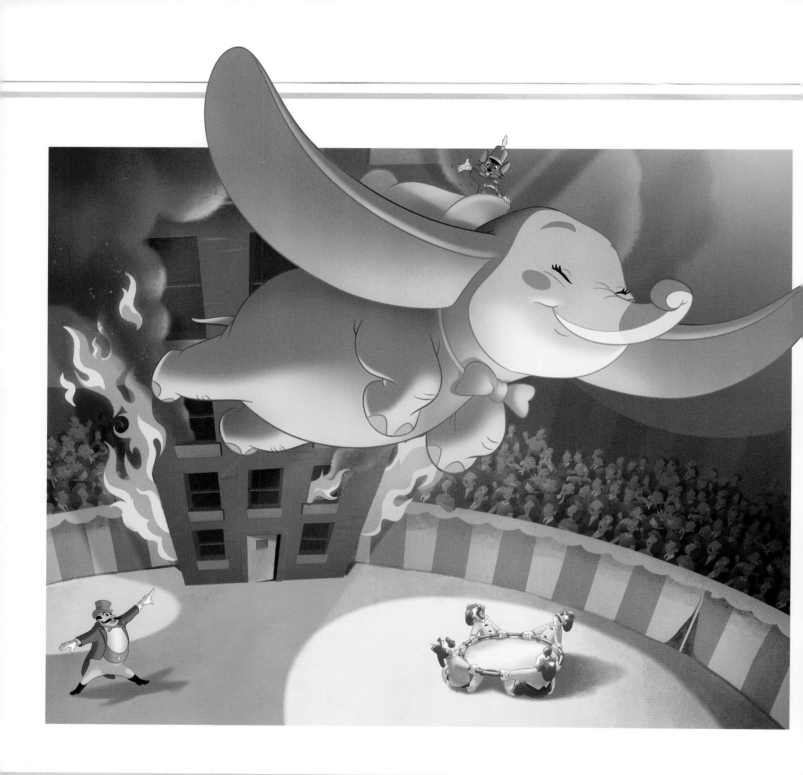

Back at the circus, Dumbo tried the clown act again. This time, as he sat at the top of the burning tower, he was ready to fly! Timothy perched inside his cap.

But just after Dumbo jumped off the tower, he lost his magic feather.

"Dumbo! Come on, fly! Open them ears!" Timothy shouted. "You can fly! Honest you can!" Dumbo suddenly got the courage he needed. He opened up his ears.

And the two friends soared high over the circus.

"Whee! We did it! We did it!" Timothy cried.

The crowds cheered. Dumbo was a star.

Dumbo became famous.

The circus was more popular than ever before. Timothy became Dumbo's manager, and he was famous, too.

And best of all, the Ringmaster freed Mrs. Jumbo. She and Dumbo even got their very own train car on the circus train. Dumbo was no longer sad. After all, there was nothing more wonderful than being with his mother again. He was now both famous and happy!

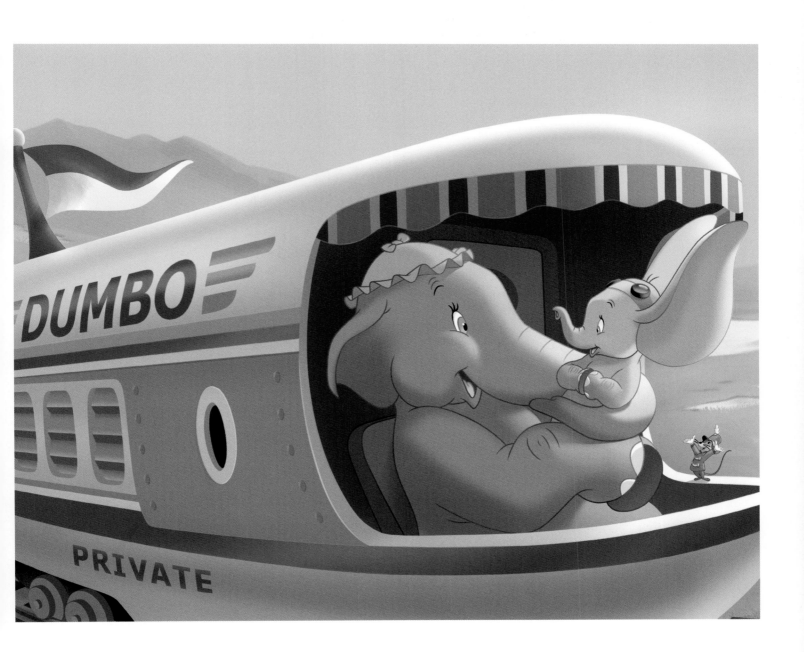

THE WONDER OF
COURAGE

"You don't need to shape-shift in order to become someone else."

—*Camilo*

ENCANTO

THE FAMILY MADRIGAL LIVED in a magical house hidden in the mountains of Colombia in a wondrous place called an Encanto.

Everyone in the family had a magical gift. Bruno's gift was the ability to see into the future, though that sometimes scared others away. Luisa had super strength. Antonio could talk to animals. Camilo could shape-shift. As for Mirabel, she had the gift to bring the whole family together and show them their worth beyond their magical gifts.

Bruno enjoyed dramatic television shows called telenovelas.

One night the Madrigals gathered to watch Bruno's latest creation: a made-up telenovela.

Bruno set up an old crate on top of a barrel. It was a little stage with his rat friends as the actors. Bruno was the narrator.

"Telenovelas are fun!" said Antonio after the show. "They make me laugh!"

"How can you laugh, Toñito?" Luisa objected, holding back tears. "They are so sad."

"I'm starting to feel a little drizzle," Pepa said. The weather was dependent on Pepa's moods. If she was feeling sad, it rained—as it did right then!

Later, Mirabel asked Bruno if he wanted to be an actor with his rats.

"You have created a wonderful telenovela with the rats," she said. "Why don't you act with them?"

"Oh, no, no, no . . . I can't act," Bruno said. "I'm not that talented."

But Mirabel had an idea. The next morning at breakfast with the Madrigal kids, she said: "Let's show Tío Bruno what a great actor he truly is. This might give him the confidence and the courage he needs to act in a telenovela!"

All the kids agreed to help. They thought it was a great idea.

"Tío Bruno," Luisa said. "I need to repair Señora Osma's wall. I was wondering if you could help me with the stucco."

"Me?" Bruno asked. "I can't! However, Jorge could." Jorge was someone Bruno could pretend to be.

Luisa smiled. Then she insisted that Bruno give it a try. Bruno courageously put a bucket on his head and changed his voice.

He was acting as Jorge!

Together, Luisa and "Jorge" fixed the wall. Bruno even lifted his bucket hat at the end when Señora Osma offered him some juice.

Later Antonio invited his uncle and his rats to play with him. Antonio wanted to go up into the trees with the jaguar.

"I'm afraid of heights," Bruno admitted. "And I don't think I could ride on a jaguar."

"You are such an amazing actor, tío!" Antonio said. "When you pretend to be Hernando, you aren't afraid of anything. I bet you could act like Hernando now!" Antonio suggested.

Bruno pulled the hood of his poncho over the top of his head. He was filled with courage. He began acting as Hernando. He raced through the trees with Antonio and the jaguar.

After he came down from the tree with Antonio and the jaguar, Bruno saw Abuela Alma.

"What is going on here?" she asked.

"Sorry," Bruno said.

Then, suddenly, Abuela transformed into Camilo. Camilo had just shape-shifted to look like Abuela to have some fun. Everyone laughed.

"My power is my way of acting," Camilo said. "But you have natural acting talent, tío! You don't need to shape-shift in order to become someone else."

Now Bruno felt even more empowered. He gathered all his courage and began to act again. He hoped Camilo could guess the character he was playing.

Bruno lifted all his rats into the air. He changed his tone of voice. He was acting as someone else as he said, "You need me to carry all of the donkeys? No problem!"

"I know who you are!" Camilo exclaimed. "Luisa!" Bruno was so excited that he shape-shifted into her, too.

Bruno was happy. He now understood that he could be anything he wanted, so long as he loved it and put his heart into it.

Later, as the family gathered for dinner, Bruno could not stop smiling. He sat next to Mirabel. It had been a very special day, filled with new experiences and wonderful moments with his family. And he had gained the courage to act in front of others.

"You should be proud," Mirabel said. "You *are* a great actor."

Alone with his rats after dinner, Bruno said, "It looks as if my other gift is acting. And I've got a brand-new idea for a telenovela with a guest star—*ME*!" He paused for a moment and added, "But first I'd better work on building a bigger stage!"

THE WONDER OF
COURAGE

"Everyone is good at something."
—*Benja*

RAYA
AND THE
LAST DRAGON

EVERY AFTERNOON, RAYA MET her father, Benja, for tea. She had been spending much of her time in training. "I'll be Guardian of the Dragon Gem soon."

"I'm proud of your hard work," Benja said, "but you must remember to make time for other things. Balance is important."

"Yes, Ba." Raya nodded.

"I have a surprise for you," Benja added, handing her a basket.

Raya peered inside to see a small armored ball.

Raya picked it up and held it in her hand. Two furry legs appeared, and a big pair of eyes looked up at her.

"His name is Tuk Tuk," said Benja. "And it will be up to you to take care of him."

Raya was delighted. The little creature was adorable, and she liked him instantly. She wasn't sure what to do first, though.

"Remember: patience and balance," said Benja. "And make sure to look for the best in him."

Raya set Tuk Tuk down and watched as he took a few clumsy steps. A beetle landed in his path and charged toward him. Alarmed, Tuk Tuk tried to get out of the strange creature's way. Instead, he accidentally flipped over and landed on his shell. As he struggled to get up, Raya said, "I gotcha."

Gently she turned him over.

"I can tell you will be great friends,"

Benja said.

"Thank you, Ba," Raya said, giving her father a hug. "I love him!"

When Raya headed back out, she tried to get Tuk Tuk to follow her. He was so distracted that Raya had to pick him up and carry him. She took him to her obstacle course. It was Raya's favorite place to train! But Tuk Tuk seemed to be distracted by all sorts of things outside the course.

He wandered about looking at flowers and spiderwebs, water pools and turtles. And Raya spent nearly all her time taking care of him, just as her father had said. But it was hard work!

Then Raya had an idea. She built a mini obstacle course just for Tuk Tuk! His first challenge was to climb some netting.

But instead, Tuk Tuk ended up chasing a butterfly.

Then he was supposed to balance on some logs.

But instead Tuk Tuk rolled and landed stuck on his back again.

Finally, Tuk Tuk was supposed to cross a long board.

But instead Tuk Tuk settled at one end of the board and fell asleep.

The next day at tea, Raya told her father about Tuk Tuk.

"I tried to give him his own mini obstacle course, but it didn't work very well. I don't know what to do, Ba," she said with a sigh.

"Be patient," said Benja. "You are still getting to know each other. Everyone is good at something. Once you figure out what Tuk Tuk is good at, you will know what to do."

Raya shrugged. Tuk Tuk seemed to be good at one thing: getting distracted!

Just then, she looked at the tea table. Tuk Tuk was eating all the dessert! He seemed to be distracted again. Or was he?

When Raya saw how focused Tuk Tuk was on his desserts, she had a new idea.

She called to Tuk Tuk, but he didn't respond. When she held up a treat, Tuk Tuk raced right over to her. Raya gave him a small piece of the treat and then walked away. Tuk Tuk followed!

Raya and Tuk Tuk returned to his mini obstacle course. Every time Tuk Tuk made it past an obstacle, Raya gave him a treat.

Tuk Tuk was officially in training. They repeated the exercises every day, and Tuk Tuk became better and better.

One day, after Tuk Tuk had zoomed past every obstacle, Raya said, "It's time."

Raya brought Tuk Tuk to the much larger obstacle course where she trained. As she began to practice, Tuk Tuk followed her!

They worked together all day and for several days afterward. They improved their skills. And Tuk Tuk got lots of treats.

Now they both were ready for their next big challenge. Raya looked at Tuk Tuk and said, "Let's do this."

Tuk Tuk had proved to be a good friend, sticking by her side through the toughest obstacles.

Now Raya put on her gloves and mask and tied her hair back. With her friend Tuk Tuk by her side, she crept into the night. Raya was ready to show she had the strength and intelligence to pass all the obstacles, reach the inner platform where the last dragon's Gem was kept, and prove herself a Guardian of the Gem.

And that was exactly what she did—with a little help from her new friend.